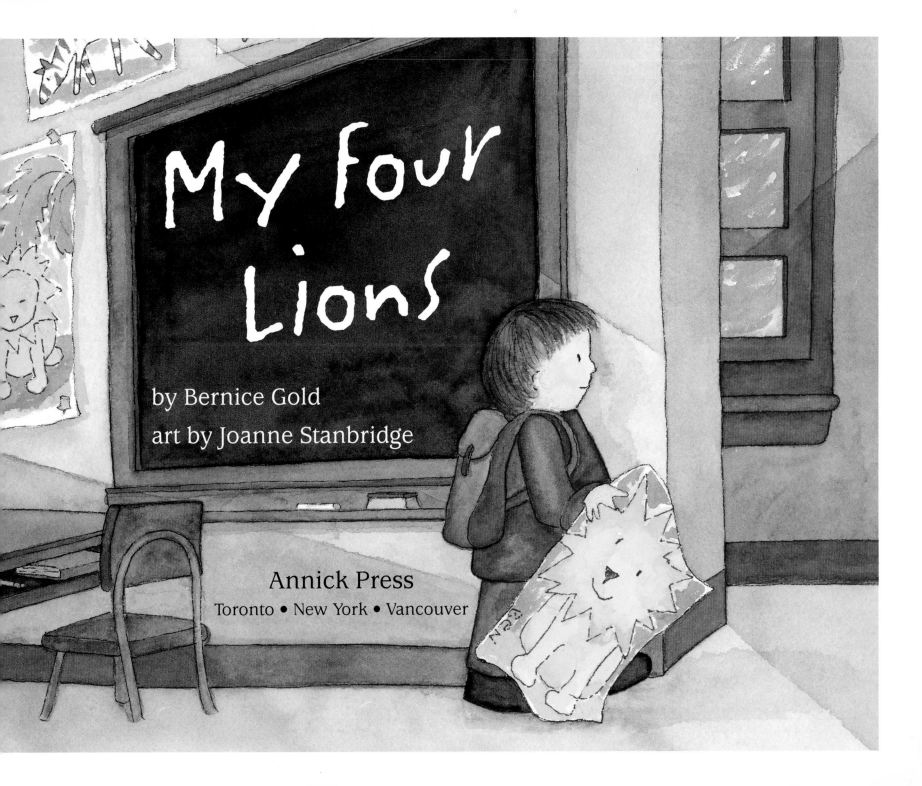

My four Lions

by Bernice Gold

art by Joanne Stanbridge

Annick Press

Toronto • New York • Vancouver

Annick Press Ltd.

We acknowledge the support of the Canada Council for the Arts for our publishing program. We also thank the Ontario Arts Council.

We acknowledge the financial support of the Government of Canada through the Book Publishing Industry Development Program for our publishing activities.

Cataloguing in Publication Data
Gold, Bernice
      My four lions

ISBN 1-55037-603-9 (bound) ISBN 1-55037-602-0 (pbk.)

I. Stanbridge, Joanne, 1960- . II. Title.

PS8563.O523M9 1999   jC813'.54   C99-930674-X
PZ7.G5813My 1999

The art in this book was rendered in watercolors. The text was typeset in Usherwood.

Distributed in Canada by: Published in the U.S.A. by Annick Press (U.S.) Ltd.
Firefly Books Ltd. Distributed in the U.S.A. by:
3680 Victoria Park Avenue Firefly Books (U.S.) Inc.
Willowdale, ON P.O. Box 1338
M2H 3K1 Ellicott Station
    Buffalo, NY 14205

Printed and bound in Canada by Friesens, Altona, Manitoba.

For Allen
And Remembering Eva
—B.G.

For my own four lions: Deb, Dian, JaneK and Nancy,
with love.
—J.S.

When I get out of school I head
straight for my camp.

I follow the path deep
into the forest.

The forest is dark,
but I'm never afraid.

'Cause my friends are there waiting,

guarding the campfire.

When I get to my camp they are so glad to see me,

they all crowd around: Angus, Pierre, Roger and Claude.

Claude is the strongest, but Angus is bigger.

Roger's the fiercest, but Pierre can shake hands.

I crawl into my tent

and bring out the pizza.

I cut five equal pieces while my friends crouch there waiting.
Then we sit around the fire and eat up our suppers.

When it gets dark I tell lion stories

to make them stay brave.

And I know when I sleep they will guard me till morning.